I LOVE RAINY DAYS!

Copyright © 2011 by Hans Wilhelm, Inc.

All rights reserved. Published by Scholastic Inc.
SCHOLASTIC, CARTWHEEL BOOKS, NOODLES, and associated logos
are trademarks and/or registered trademarks of Scholastic Inc.
Lexile is a registered trademark of MetaMetrics, Inc.

Library of Congress Cataloging-in-Publication Data is available.

ISBN 978-0-545-24503-6

12 11 10 9 8 7 6 5 4 3 2 1   10 11 12 13 14 15/0

Printed in the U.S.A. 40 • First printing, March 2011

noodles®

SCHOLASTIC READER
LEVEL 1
50-250 WORDS

I LOVE RAINY DAYS!

by Hans Wilhelm

Cartwheel
·B·O·O·K·S·®

SCHOLASTIC INC.

New York   Toronto   London   Auckland
Sydney   Mexico City   New Delhi   Hong Kong

I hate rain.
I want to
play outside.

I am bored!

Wait!
I have an idea.

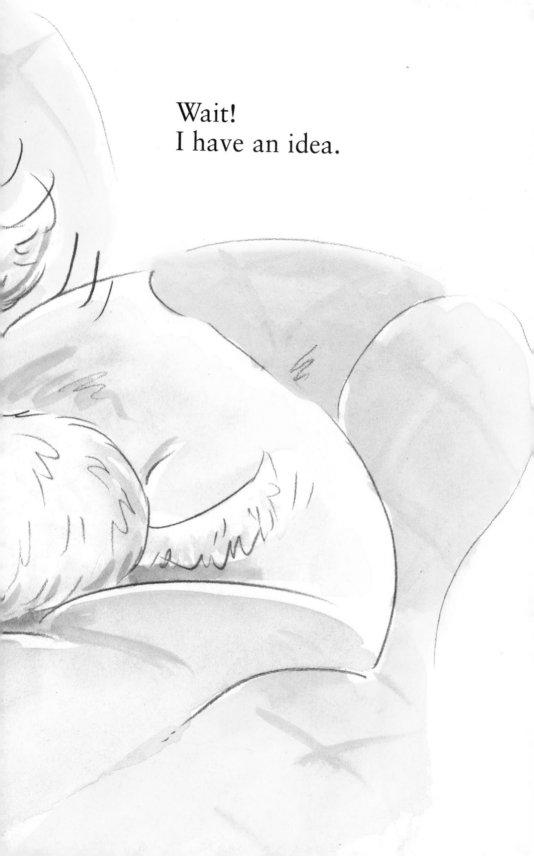

I can play tag!

I can go for a ride.

I can taste the cookies.

I can play games.

I can hide my bone.

I can make art on the carpet.

I can help empty the trash.

I can give Teddy a workout.

I can unroll the paper.

I'm tired.
That was a very busy day!

I need a nap.

I love rainy days!